*The Magical
Rainbow Series continues
with this space adventure of how
the Magical Rainbow Man becomes
a messenger of Love for Planet Earth.*

THE MISSING MAGICAL ENERGY

STORY AND ART THROUGH SHAHASTRA

The Magical Rainbow Man Publications

Dear Friends:

As a guide and a friend to our children, I feel that we have been given the position of nurturing and inspiring their highest attributes. We can surround our children with a loving atmosphere, good associations and sound tools for living. Books are very important tools we all can use every day to expand learning and awareness.

The Magical Rainbow Man Publications is a family company. We are bringing forth books to encourage the qualities of caring, giving, cooperating and sharing. We have created new heroes with positive values to inspire children of all ages to care more about our planet. In re-creating an innocence and beauty that seems so lost in a child's world today, we wish to give them hope for the future and the vision to make Earth a better place to live.

We thank you for supporting these efforts and for being a concerned individual in order to bring forth a generation of truly loving and giving children.

The Magical Rainbow Man

"Wholly positive books. Certain to capture children's imagination . . . and serve as an inspiration to see colors of the world around them in a new way. Permeated by magic and a sense of awe. I cannot imagine more inspiring books for a parent to share with a child of any age."

Mark Rosin,
Writer and Senior Editor,
Parent's Magazine

Box 717 • Ojai, California 93023

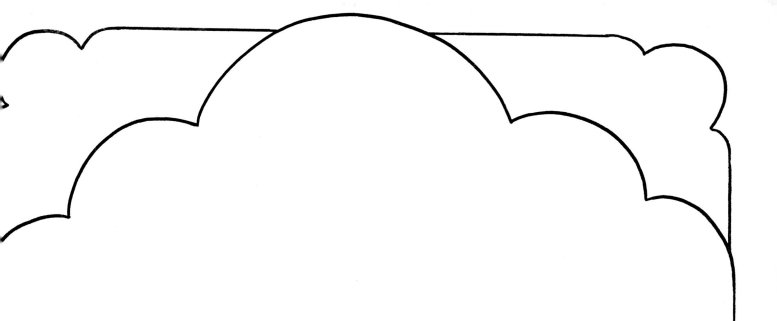

THE MAGICAL RAINBOW MAN AND THE JOURNEY OF LOVE

An illustrated story through Shahastra

This book is part of the Magical Rainbow
Series of inspiring and educational journeys
into secret enchanting worlds. Come
with us on this magical adventure!

THE MAGICAL RAINBOW MAN

and the Journey of Love

an illustrated story through
Shahastra

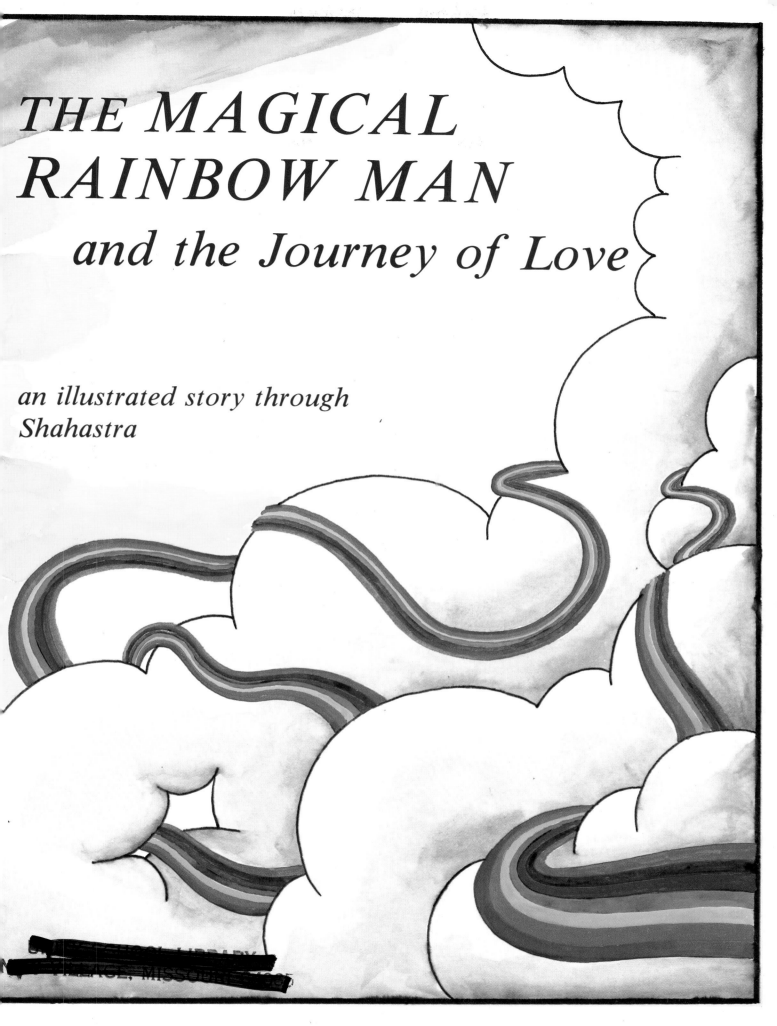

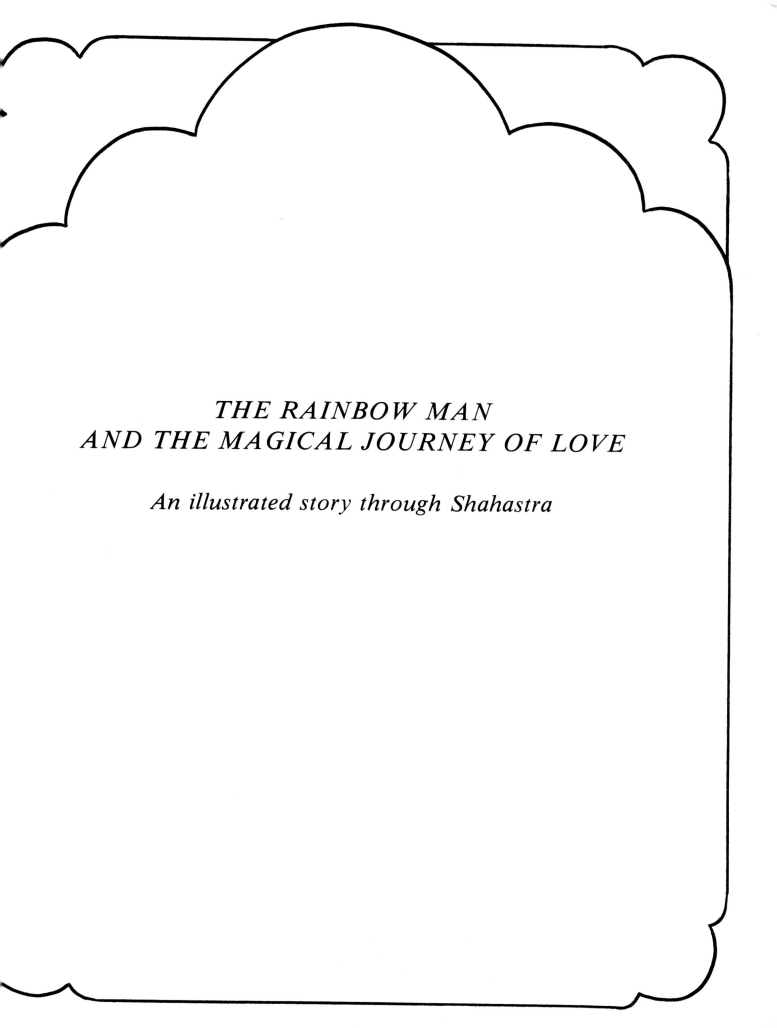

THE RAINBOW MAN
AND THE MAGICAL JOURNEY OF LOVE

An illustrated story through Shahastra

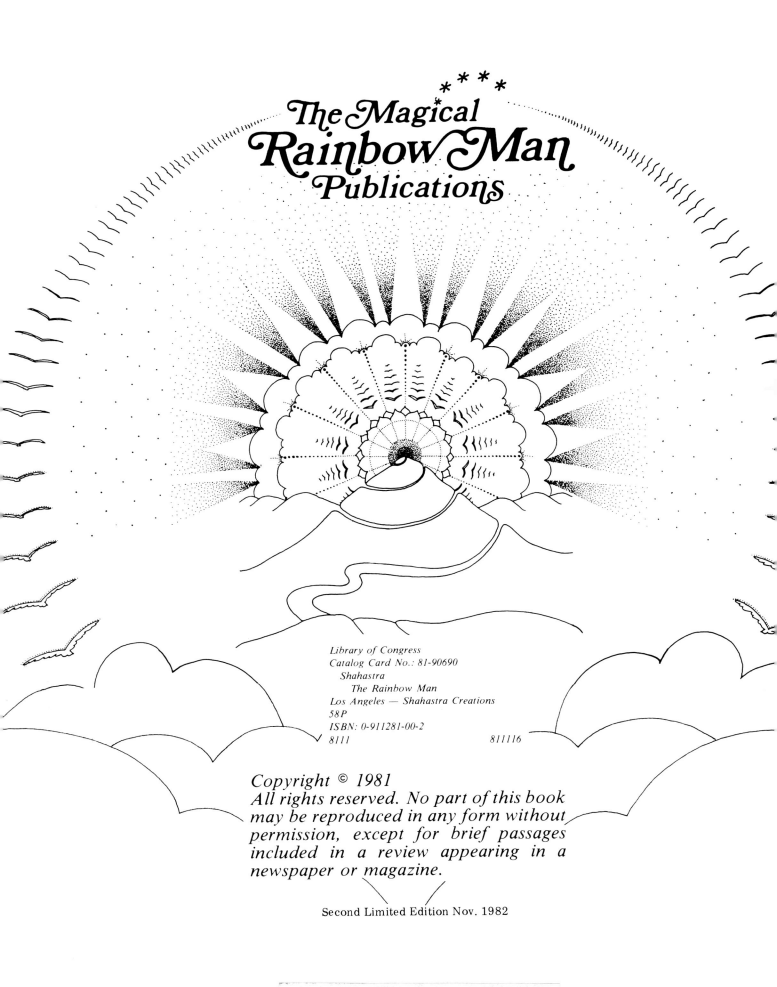

The Magical Rainbow Man Publications

Library of Congress
Catalog Card No.: 81-90690
Shahastra
The Rainbow Man
Los Angeles — Shahastra Creations
58P
ISBN: 0-911281-00-2
8111   *811116*

Second Limited Edition Nov. 1982

BOX 717. OJAI, CALIFORNIA 93023

Dedicated to all the
beautiful children who have been
waiting patiently for the
wonderful Rainbow Man.

It is said that the Rainbow Man comes from the skies whenever there is a moment of love on earth. He is a magical being who especially loves children and brings with him all the beautiful colors as gifts to give.

One afternoon, as Misha, Jacob and Zandra were playing in the park, the Rainbow Man appeared.

"Do you hear that?" Jacob wondered, hearing first a soft tinkling, like glass bells ringing, and then a harp song that sounded as if an angel in heaven was playing.

"Look!" exclaimed Misha.

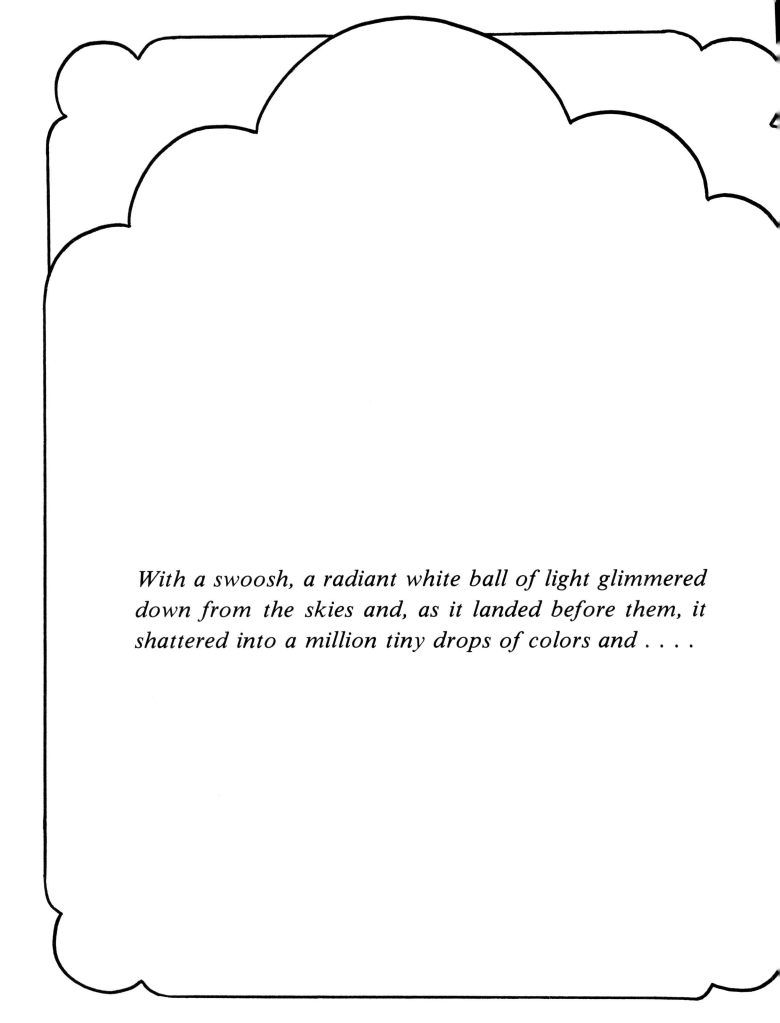

With a swoosh, a radiant white ball of light glimmered down from the skies and, as it landed before them, it shattered into a million tiny drops of colors and . . . .

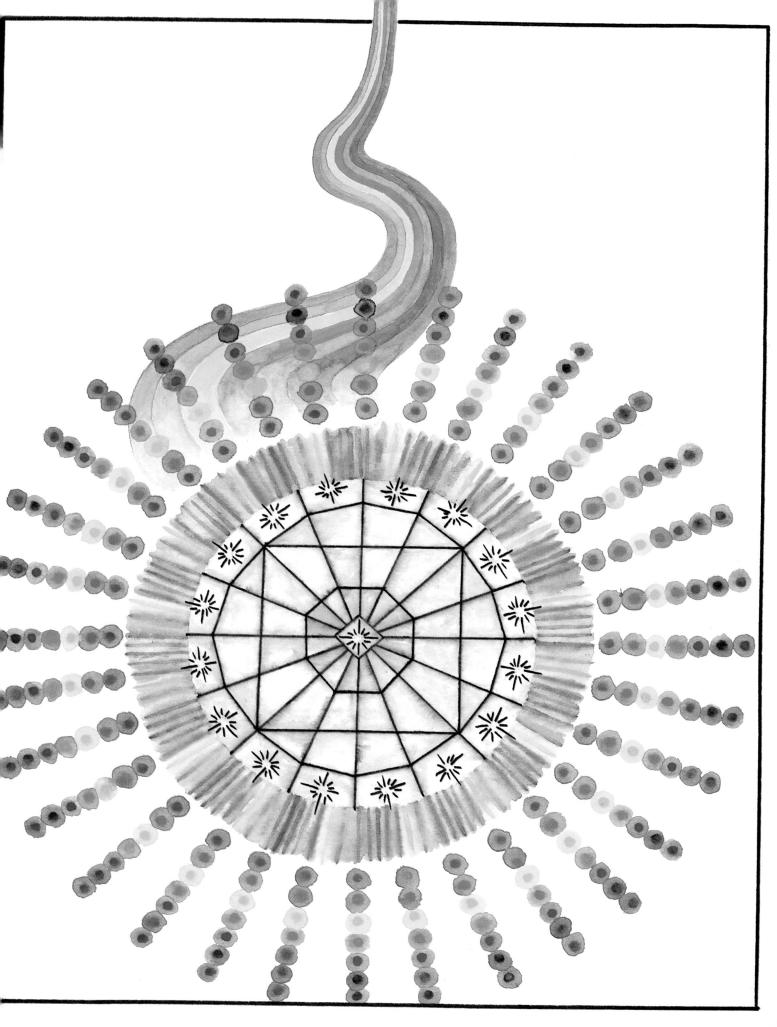

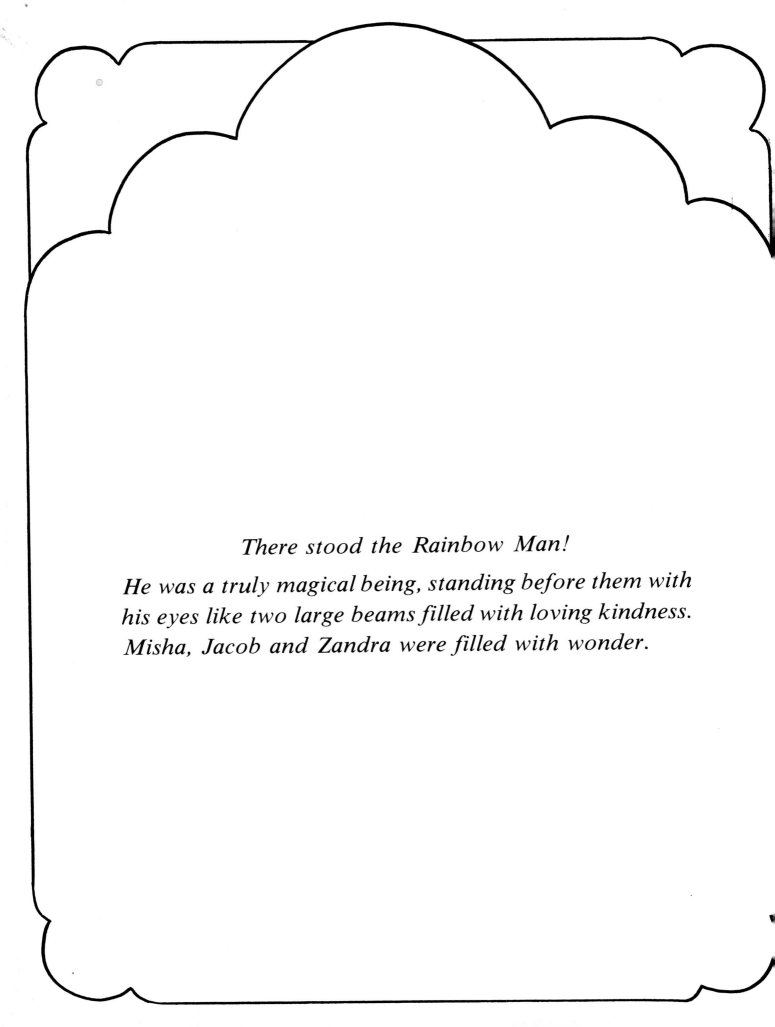

There stood the Rainbow Man!

He was a truly magical being, standing before them with his eyes like two large beams filled with loving kindness. Misha, Jacob and Zandra were filled with wonder.

"I wish to take you to the Land of Colorful Love," he said softly and scooped up the children in his wide billowy arms. He must have known already that they had wanted to go but they were too amazed to even speak.

Together they sailed up to the sky on wafts of cool blue air. Up, Up, Up through a blur of whiteness—

"Oh, we're in the clouds!" Zandra cried.

And, there, shining with great majesty and splendor, was the most exquisite rainbow the children had ever seen.

"O-o-o-o," marveled the three, their eyes opened wide.

"I want you to meet the seven beings who are in charge of the rainbow colors. They will teach you many wonderful things," said the Rainbow Man.

As the Rainbow Man spoke, a soft red mist began to surround them and the children felt all glowy and warm. From out of the lighted mist, a beautiful being appeared.

"I am the Queen of the Land of Red.
Red is the color of strength," she said.
"When there is love in your heart, let it be strong.
And let it keep growing all day long."
"A love Queen!" whispered Misha.

The Rainbow Man's eyes gleamed as he whisked the three into the next color land. A brilliant orange surrounded them and a being was seated before them glittering like a jewel.

"I am the Goddess of the Orange Land here.
Orange gives you energy when you fear.
Let not your heart be afraid to give,
For it's only with giving you learn to live."
"Orange is my favorite color," declared Jacob.

The Rainbow Man took them into a bright yellow color
like the land of a big sun where a winged being knelt upon
a flash of a flower.

"I am the Fairy of this gleaming Yellow Land.
Yellow brightens your mind to understand.
When you understand how bright love is
Your mind will open in joy and bliss."

"What a cheerful color!" exclaimed Zandra.

Then the Rainbow Man led them to a cooler green land.
It felt like a deep cool leafy forest and a calm smiling
being greeted them.

"I am the Maiden of the Land of Green.
Green gives harmony to every living being.
It soothes the heart so deep inside
And gives you a loving smile so wide."
"Green feels good," said Misha.

Further into the rainbow they all drifted, coming upon the bluest space the children had ever seen. A being of radiant blue approached them.

"I am the Deva of the Land of Blue
Blue is a peaceful color flowing through.
When you're full of peace you love all things
And know what joy and beauty brings."

"She is beautiful!" whispered Jacob.

The blue changed slowly to a deep violet-blue color, like a late evening sky just after the first stars come out.

"This color is indigo," explained the Rainbow Man. "A truly rare color to know and here is the guardian of this ray." As he spoke, a violet-blue being emerged ever so quietly.

"I am the Angel of the Land of Indigo.
Indigo gives wisdom so you may know
To hear your inner voice that ◊ tells you all,
To use your inner light to ◊ love your world."

"That *is* a special color,"
Zandra said.

"And now to the last color land," smiled the Rainbow Man. He looked so beautiful with his eyes gleaming. A radiant violet surrounded them as a mystical being appeared before them.

"I am the Spirit of this Violet Land bright
Violet opens your soul to see the Light
And when you open to the Cosmic Light of Love
Everything is One both below and above."

"Like one loving Universe!" exclaimed Misha.

"Now you must return," all the beings said.
"Go back to your world of yellow, green and red,
Of violet and orange and indigo and blue
And remember these colors that speak to you.
And whenever you see a rainbow in the sky above
Remember it is telling you all to Love."

The Rainbow Man glided the children into his arms and flashed down toward the earth. Misha, Jacob and Zandra felt as if their hearts were filled with colored sparkling jewels and they were racing toward home to give them all away. Such treasures they had!

"So you see, my children," smiled the Rainbow Man, as they landed, "It is not so hard for you to love each other here on earth. But everyone has forgotten, haven't they?"

"We can help them remember!" exclaimed Misha joyfully.

"Yes, you can help," the Rainbow Man's eyes twinkled. "Do you know what happens when people see rainbows?"

"They always say, 'Oh, how beautiful!'" remarked Jacob.

"Yes," said the Rainbow Man, "and suddenly their hearts open and they feel how truly beautiful they are and everyone else and the whole world."

The Rainbow Man gathered the children into his arms and spoke very softly. "You've learned much about love from the beings of the rainbow."

"But a rainbow doesn't appear in the sky every day to remind the people," said Zandra.

*"So **you** must be like little rainbows," replied the Rainbow Man, "Colors of love to shine upon all you meet."*

"And just in case **you** forget," he said, as he pulled a tiny cloth bag from his pocket, "I will give you each a rainbow of your own that will always remind you."

He gave them each a beautiful sparkling crystal to hang in their window.

"O-O-O-h!" they all murmured.

"Now when the sun peeks through your window every morning and sends a beam through the crystal, you'll see the rainbow dancing on your wall. Then you will remember."

Misha, Jacob and Zandra each hugged the Rainbow Man.

"Thank you, thank you for the wonderful voyage," Misha said.

"And the magical crystal," Jacob added.

"And...we love you," whispered Zandra.

"I must go now," the Rainbow Man declared. He started to float up towards the sky into a gossamer multi-colored mist. He was so beautiful!

"Goodbye, goodbye!" the children waved, *"We'll miss you!"*

*"Oh, one more thing!" he called down to them, smiling.
"When it is cloudy and you can't see a rainbow anywhere,
that is the best time to love."*

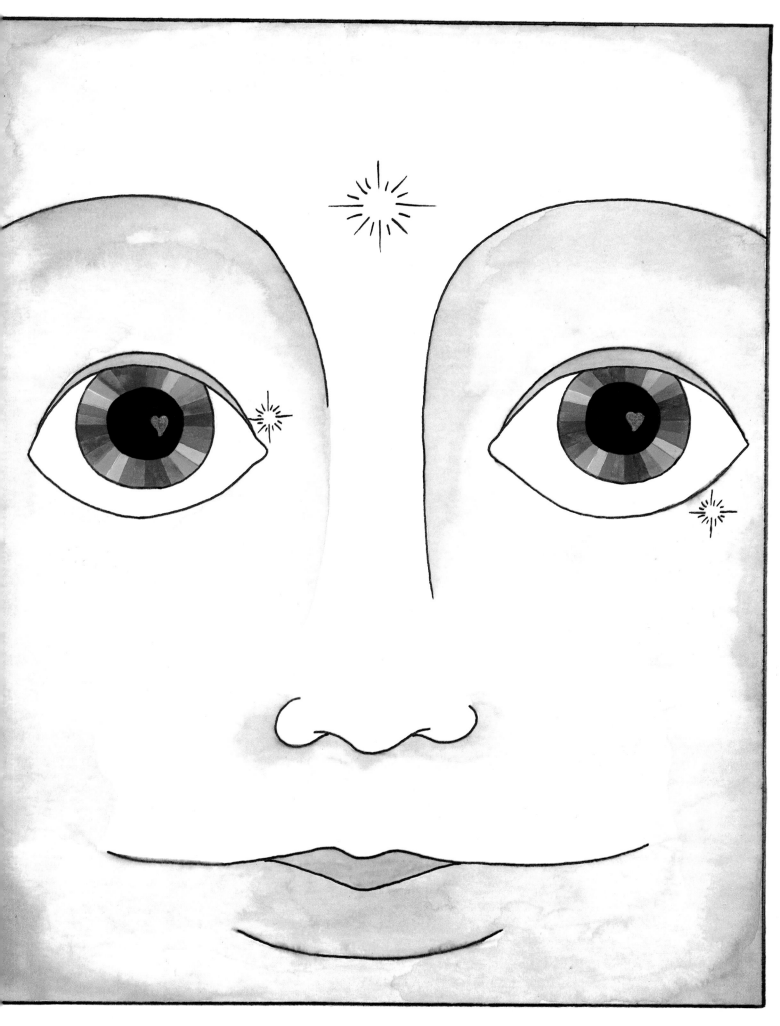

Here's a page for you to color and cut out.

Also, if you'd like to be one of my special rainbow helpers and know all about my new adventures, I'll keep you informed with my Secret Magical Scroll.

I be waiting to hear from you!
Love,
The Rainbow Man

Name _____

Address _____

City _____

State_____ Zip _____

Send for the Magical Rainbow Man *full-color Poster*, 19 x 22".
$3.00 plus $1.00 shipping/handling plus 6% sales tax for Calif. residents only
or
Send $2.50 plus $1.00 shipping/handling plus 6% sales tax for Calif. residents only for your *Magical Scroll* with a special magical rainbow sticker to:
The Magical Rainbow Man
Box 717
Ojai, CA 93023

The *Magical*
Rainbow Man
****

Box 717
Ojai.Ca.93023

The *Magical*
Rainbow Man
****

Box 717
Ojai.Ca.93023

The *Magical*
Rainbow Man
****

Box 717
Ojai.Ca.93023

The *Magical*
Rainbow Man
****

Box 717
Ojai.Ca.93023

MAGICAL RAINBOW HELPER CLUB

Join hands with me to help make Earth a more beautiful place to live. If you send your name and address, I will make you one of my special Rainbow Helpers (and I need a **lot** of help!) To join is free and if you send a **self-addressed, stamped envelope,** you will receive **3** Rainbow crystal heart stickers to spread more magical love upon Planet Earth.

Also, I would love to hear from you! Tell me what you are doing to make Earth a better place for us all to live and let me know how you and your parents feel about the books.

Love,

The Magical Rainbow Man

Please send me:

- ☐ Magical Scrolls @ $2.00 plus $1.00 postage and handling
- ☐ Magical Rainbow Man Poster @ $3.00 plus $1.00 postage and handling
- ☐ Missing Magical Energy Poster (A rainbow space poster) @ $3.00 plus $1.00 postage and handling
- ☐ Magical Rainbow Man T-Shirt Iron-on Decal $2.00 plus $1.00 shipping

PLUS 6% Sales Tax California only

Name (please print) _____

Address _____

City _____ State _____ Zip _____

GIVE THIS CARD TO A FRIEND TO JOIN.

MAGICAL RAINBOW HELPER CLUB

Join hands with me to help make Earth a more beautiful place to live. If you send your name and address, I will make you one of my special Rainbow Helpers (and I need a **lot** of help!) To join is free and if you send a **self-addressed, stamped envelope,** you will receive **3** Rainbow crystal heart stickers to spread more magical love upon Planet Earth.

Also, I would love to hear from you! Tell me what you are doing to make Earth a better place for us all to live and let me know how you and your parents feel about the books.

Love,

The Magical Rainbow Man

Please send me:

- ☐ Magical Scrolls @ $2.00 plus $1.00 postage and handling
- ☐ Magical Rainbow Man Poster @ $3.00 plus $1.00 postage and handling
- ☐ Missing Magical Energy Poster (A rainbow space poster) @ $3.00 plus $1.00 postage and handling
- ☐ Magical Rainbow Man T-Shirt Iron-on Decal $2.00 plus $1.00 shipping

PLUS 6% Sales Tax California only

Name (please print) _____

Address _____

City _____ State _____ Zip _____

GIVE THIS CARD TO A FRIEND TO JOIN.

MAGICAL RAINBOW HELPER CLUB

Join hands with me to help make Earth a more beautiful place to live. If you send your name and address, I will make you one of my special Rainbow Helpers (and I need a **lot** of help!) To join is free and if you send a **self-addressed, stamped envelope,** you will receive **3** Rainbow crystal heart stickers to spread more magical love upon Planet Earth.

Also, I would love to hear from you! Tell me what you are doing to make Earth a better place for us all to live and let me know how you and your parents feel about the books.

Love,

The Magical Rainbow Man

Please send me:

- ☐ Magical Scrolls @ $2.00 plus $1.00 postage and handling
- ☐ Magical Rainbow Man Poster @ $3.00 plus $1.00 postage and handling
- ☐ Missing Magical Energy Poster (A rainbow space poster) @ $3.00 plus $1.00 postage and handling
- ☐ Magical Rainbow Man T-Shirt Iron-on Decal $2.00 plus $1.00 shipping

PLUS 6% Sales Tax California only

Name (please print) _____

Address _____

City _____ State _____ Zip _____

GIVE THIS CARD TO A FRIEND TO JOIN.

MAGICAL RAINBOW HELPER CLUB

Join hands with me to help make Earth a more beautiful place to live. If you send your name and address, I will make you one of my special Rainbow Helpers (and I need a **lot** of help!) To join is free and if you send a **self-addressed, stamped envelope,** you will receive **3** Rainbow crystal heart stickers to spread more magical love upon Planet Earth.

Also, I would love to hear from you! Tell me what you are doing to make Earth a better place for us all to live and let me know how you and your parents feel about the books.

Love,

The Magical Rainbow Man

Please send me:

- ☐ Magical Scrolls @ $2.00 plus $1.00 postage and handling
- ☐ Magical Rainbow Man Poster @ $3.00 plus $1.00 postage and handling
- ☐ Missing Magical Energy Poster (A rainbow space poster) @ $3.00 plus $1.00 postage and handling
- ☐ Magical Rainbow Man T-Shirt Iron-on Decal $2.00 plus $1.00 shipping

PLUS 6% Sales Tax California only

Name (please print) _____

Address _____

City _____ State _____ Zip _____

GIVE THIS CARD TO A FRIEND TO JOIN.